DI

NORMAN
PRICE

BELLA
LASAGNE

JAMES

SARAH

MEET ALL THESE FRIENDS IN BUZZ BOOKS:

Thomas the Tank Engine
The Animals of Farthing Wood
Biker Mice from Mars
Winnie-the-Pooh
Fireman Sam
Rupert
Babar

First published in Great Britain 1990 by Buzz Books
an imprint of Reed Children's Books
Michelin House, 81 Fulham Road, London SW3 6RB
and Auckland, Melbourne, Singapore and Toronto
Reprinted 1992, 1995

Fireman Sam copyright © 1985 Prism Art & Design Limited
Text and illustrations copyright © 1990 Reed International Books Limited
Based on the animation series produced by Bumper Films for
S4C/Channel 4 Wales and Prism Art & Design Limited
Original idea by Dave Gingell and Dave Jones, assisted by Mike Young
Characters created by Rob Lee
All rights reserved

ISBN 1 85591 033 0

Printed and bound in Italy by Olivotto

CHRISTMAS IN PONTYPANDY

Story by Caroline Hill-Trevor
Illustrations by CLIC!

When the people of Pontypandy woke on Christmas Eve there was a surprise for them. It had snowed heavily during the night and now the village was glistening in the sun. "Magic," shouted Norman, as he ran out of the shop. "See you later, Mam. I'm off sledging."

"Norman!" shouted Dilys, looking round.
"Come back here and help me clear the
path." But Norman had run off down the
street with his sledge.

James and Sarah were making a snowman.

"The finishing touch!" grinned James,
placing an old cap on the snowman's head.

"He looks just like Trevor," Sarah giggled.
"Oh, hello, Trevor, didn't see you there.
What do you think of our snowman?"

Trevor laughed. "Very handsome!"

Norman came tearing up the road.
"Come on, you two, bring your sledge. I'll
race you down the mountain!"

"A hundred miles an hour!" cried James,
and the three children set off with their
sledges towards the hillside overlooking
Pontypandy.

At Pontypandy Fire Station, the firefighters
had cleared all the snow from the drive so
Jupiter, the fire engine, could get away
quickly if there was an emergency call.

Fireman Sam?'' said Station Officer Steele.

"No, Sir," agreed Fireman Sam, "but let's hope we're in for a quiet day. We've got to go and fetch the Christmas tree for the village square.''

11

Outside the village, Sarah, James and Norman were having fun sledging.

"Weeeee!" squealed Sarah, as she and James shot down the hill.

"Let's try over there," suggested Norman, pointing at a much steeper slope. "We could beat the world snow speed record!"

"I don't think . . ." said James, as they trudged up to the top of the steepest hill. "It's very steep."

"Come on, scaredy cat," jeered Sarah. "Let's show him we can do it!"

"One, two, three, GO!" shouted Norman,
and off they went, faster and faster,
gathering speed over the smooth snow.

Norman was in the lead.

"First one through the gate is the
winner," he yelled, as he shot between the
gateposts. "Yes! It's the gold for Norman
Price! Magic!"

"Look out!" cried Sarah, as the sledges sped on. "We're heading straight for the pond." Norman rolled off his sledge into a snowdrift. "Brake, James, brake!" screamed Sarah, but their sledge was going too fast.

15

It reached the bottom of the hill and shot across the ice to the centre of the pond. There was a loud CRACK! "The ice is breaking," gasped Sarah in horror.

"We'll drown!" screamed James.

"Don't move," yelled Norman. "I'll go and 'phone for help," and he ran off towards Pandy Lane, leaving Sarah and James clinging to their sledge in the centre of the pond.

At Pontypandy Fire Station, the alarm rang out and a message came through on the printer. "Children trapped on ice in middle of Pandy Pond," read Station Officer Steele. A few seconds later, the firefighters were on their way in Jupiter.

"Great fires of London! It's Sarah and James," cried Fireman Sam, when they reached the pond. "Don't panic, you two."

"Save us, Uncle Sam!" shouted James.
  The firefighters placed a ladder on the ground and carefully extended it over the ice towards the children.

"Now then, Sarah," called Fireman Sam.
"Come towards me slowly, on all fours.
Wait a minute, James."

"O.K., Uncle Sam," said James, bravely.

21

Sarah crawled along the ladder to the edge
of the ice, and a few moments later she was
standing safely on the bank. "Your turn
now, James," said Fireman Sam. Soon
James too was safe on the ground again.

"Right then," said Fireman Sam. "Let's get you three warm and dry. Come on."

Sarah, James and Norman climbed into Jupiter with the firefighters and they set off back to Pontypandy.

Bella soon had the children warming themselves in front of the fire. "These baked potatoes are great for warming you up when you come back from an arctic expedition," said James.

"If it hadn't been for Norman, you

wouldn't be back at all," said Fireman Sam.
"Snow is great fun to play in, but ice can be
very dangerous. You should only sledge
where you know it's safe," he warned.

"Thanks, Norman," said Sarah.

"O.K.," mumbled Norman, bashfully.

As darkness fell on the village the snow
made everything look magical. "This is a
great Christmas tree, Uncle Sam," said James
as everyone gathered round to sing carols.

26

Fireman Sam produced a large sack and
spoke to the twins. "I'm working on
Christmas Day, so you'd better have these
now." He reached into the sack. "There's
one for you too, Norman."

"Thanks a million," they cried excitedly.

"Just one more thing to do," said
Fireman Sam, as he finished his cocoa later
that night. "Might as well, just in case."
And he hung his Christmas stocking on the
mantelpiece.

He looked out of the window at the snow-covered village, sparkling in the moonlight.

"Merry Christmas, Pontypandy!"

FIREMAN SAM

STATION OFFICER
STEELE

TREVOR EVANS

ELVIS
CRIDLINGTON

PENNY MORRIS